BLUE ORB CHRONICLES

By: Peter Hamble

CONTENTS

CHAPTER ONE

The Invitation

*F*rom the time he was knee high, Peter knew he was special. Praised as gifted by his parents and teacher he always knew he possessed incredible potential. Kind. Handsome. Athletic. Intelligent. It seemed that Peter had it all. And he did. But he also had a little more. Something so subtle and seemingly harmless that few could predict the suffering it would bring him. Peter had a limitless imagination and a hunger for greatness.

Now, there is nothing wrong with wanting to improve yourself, but one must be careful when allowing unrestrained fantasies to fuse with desire. More damage has been done by seemingly innocent dreams getting out of hand than by the most brutal of hardships. But we'll get to that later. For now, let us enter the wholesome world of Peter Wheatman and the simple life he lived in the village of Hamble, a small farming community where people still mended their clothes by hand and sat in candle light when the sun went down. There was a gentle magic to this place, one far different to the advanced magics that had brought the nearby megakingdom of Tropolis the great prosperity it now enjoyed. Apart from Mr. Silverman, no one from Hamble had been to Tropolis. Perhaps this was the reason that in their relative poverty, the people of Hamble were blissfully happy.

It was just another day in the Wheatman house. After rising from their beds at sunrise, Peter and his parents gathered in their cold living room beside the embers of last night's fire.

Joining hands, they prayed together in a circle. They asked for a good day, for a long happy life filled with friends and family and for everyone in the village to maintain their good health. When their good intentions were said his mother hugged and kissed them, "Now you boys work up an appetite. I'm going to be making a special bread today. Mrs. Carpenter gave me some tasty seeds yesterday and I know how you like them."

"Sure thing, mum," said Peter, "Yesterday I planted thirteen rows of wheat. Today I want to do fifteen."

"Don't kill yourself, kid," said his father in a calm and steady voice grounded in the rhythms of nature, "They'll always be more planting that needs to be done. You work at your own pace."

"This is my own pace," beamed Peter, "Planting wheat is fun." His father chuckled, "Okay, kid. Then let's get going."

In the fields Peter and his father worked in joyful silence. When his father worked, he gave his total attention to the act of planting wheat.

He spread the seeds as evenly as possible paying close attention to any area that received too many or two few. When he was satisfied with their distribution he gently ran his hand over the area, sweeping a protective layer of soil over the seeds. On the rare occasion that his mind wandered from the task at hand, his thoughts were about how much water the seeds would need or how to get it if it was a dry summer.

Peter's thoughts were far more sensational. While his physical body planted wheat, his mind travelled to distant lands. One moment he'd be in a jungle, fighting monsters and saving princesses. The next he was a powerful Warlock conjuring magnificent artwork with his powerful magecraft. In his fantasies everything was effortless. He could slay a dragon with a single arrow or summon a bolt of lightning with the click of his fingers. He never thought about his creations in detail, only that they were finished and they were perfect.

When Peter burst through the front door he was greeted by the delightful smell of freshly baked bread and the sizzling of eggs frying in a pan. His mother had diligently and with total devotion made their breakfast like she always did. On rainy days when it was too wet to work the lands Peter would help her. He could watch for hours as she kneaded the dough, mesmerized by her perfect technique, with a rhythm and grace so effortless it looked as though the bread was kneading itself. Even Peter's most determined attempts fell short of imitating her.

"Guess how many I planted today?" exclaimed Peter. "Well it sounds like you got your fifteen, honey." "Nope. Sixteen, mum. I did sixteen!"

She laughed and shook her head, "You never fail to amaze me. You put your mind to anything and nothing can stop you." Peter beamed, allowing himself to fully soak up the compliment as visions of godly achievements flashed before him.

It took several minutes before his father casually strolled through the door, "You just don't stop, do ya, kid?" he chuckled, moving to the sink and washing the dirt from his hands.

The three of them sat around the table and said grace before breakfast. Everything on the table had been made in Hamble. The bread and eggs from their own farm and they had traded some grain with the neighbour for the butter.

"You know son, it's coming up to your eighteenth birthday," said his father, "Do you have any idea how you want to spend the next year of your life?" A thousand dreams of greatness flashed through Peter's mind. And he wanted all of them. But it was not the type of desire most people feel. Peter lived with so much joy that the idea of needing anything was foreign to him. After all, how can one want anything when you feel complete? Whenever he dreamed he felt like he already possessed that which he dreamed about. If he never received it so be it, there was always another dream waiting around the corner and that wasn't going to stop anytime soon. "Nothing comes to mind," said Peter. What he meant was nothing specific comes to mind. A thousand dreams came to his mind but none was so prominent as to command his attention above all the others.

After breakfast, Peter changed out of his work clothes and left for school. He marched and whistled for a while, until a sudden jolt of energy overcame him. He took off sprinting and before he knew it, he was outside the school gate hands on his knees, panting, grinning. His face was a flush healthy red. When he caught his breath, he straightened up and waltzed inside.

In the classroom Peter oscillated between being a well behaved student and causing the occasional disruption or two. One moment he was fully engaged with the teacher, taking notes, giving answers and asking a plethora of questions. The next he was chatting with his classmates, telling jokes and finding humour in the school work. This would occasionally result in a few of his fellow students bursting into uncontrollable laughter as Mr. Silverman reprimanded Peter while trying to keep a straight face.

"Sorry," Peter would say sheepishly, then immediately repair the situation by asking Mr. Silverman a question about where they left off. At the end of the school day, when the classroom had been tidied and the students were leaving, Mr. Silverman told Peter, "Stay behind for a few minutes Peter. I need to tell you something."

"Strange," thought Peter. This was quite uncharacteristic of his teacher. When the room was empty Peter approached him, "Yes, sir?"

"You don't need me to tell you what a bright and talented young man you are," said Mr. Silverman, with an air of pride and admiration. "This isn't something I'd recommend for most people," he continued, " But you have a great many gifts and it would be a shame for you not to have an opportunity to develop them."

Peter listened carefully. "Have you ever considered studying magic?" Magic! Half of Peter's life had revolved around fantasies where he was a great Warlock of some sort or another.

"Once or twice, sir. But I've never really thought about how I would do it." Mr. Silverman smiled, "Well then. You're in luck. There are hundreds of academies in Tropolis teaching every kind of magic you can imagine. And every single one of them would be delighted to have a man like you among them."

Peter blushed, "You think so, sir?"

"I know so. I met a great many people in my time at the Informos Academy of Higher Magic and not one of them was near half as talented as you." He curled his hand into a fist and affectionately pushed it against Peter's chin, "You're a real gem, Peter."

Peter was unsure what to say. "Can I think about it, sir?"

"Of course, of course. And remember, you don't have to go. A man like you could spend his whole life in Hamble and enjoy every minute of it. I just felt you deserved to know what was out there, so that you can make an informed decision about your future."

As he walked home from school, Peter was accompanied by a potent mix of nervousness and excitement. He rarely felt anything other than euphoria, but the possibility of going to Tropolis, of stepping into the unknown brought a strange uneasiness. He wrestled with the idea in his mind examining it carefully from every angle.

"What would I gain by going to Tropolis?" he thought. "Certainly, it would be an adventure. I'd meet new people. See new places. And discover all kinds of magic."

"Yes," he countered, "But do I really need to? Life is perfect here in Hamble. I've got a loving family. Wonderful friends. And everyday I wake up happy and excited to do something I love doing. Is it really worth risking all this for the chance to explore the world?"

"It wouldn't be much of a risk. If I don't like it in Tropolis I can always return. The village loves me and would welcome me back with open arms. I could give it a one month trial. Worse case scenario I lose a month of my life. In exchange, I'm guaranteed to satisfy my curiosity."

"But there are other risks. There could be dark magic in Tropolis. Magic I can't even imagine. It could be lurking in Tropolis as I speak watching me from afar and beckoning me to come to it."

"It's possible. But Mr. Silverman didn't give any hints that dark magic would cause me any trouble. And besides, haven't I always wondered how incredible it would feel to become the world's most powerful Warlock? If I go to Tropolis, that dream could become a reality.

Think of how proud I would feel? Think of how proud my parents and Mr. Silverman and the rest of the village would be? They'd tell stories about me for a thousand years to come. I'll never be a great Warlock if I spend the rest of my life in Hamble."

"But everyone is already proud of me. I have a great life here. Who cares if people say good things about me a hundred years after I'm dead. Maybe my dreams aren't meant to become reality. Maybe they're perfect just as dreams."

Peter waited for a counter argument but the thought never came. "Well," he sighed half disappointed, half relieved, "It looks like I'm staying in Hamble."

At that moment, he realized how slowly his thoughts had made him walk. "It must be time for dinner," he thought and took off sprinting, forgetting all about Tropolis and returning to his normal, happy life.

CHAPTER TWO

Just For A Week

$\mathcal{M}$r. Silverman couldn't have been more supportive when Peter told him his decision. "It's probably for the best." he said, "The magic in Tropolis can do strange things to even the brightest of minds." The statement had aroused some curiosity in Peter, but as he had decided to stay in Hamble, he felt no need to probe deeper.

Months passed and Peter's life remained the same. In the mornings he worked the fields with his father, in the afternoons he went to school and joked with his friends, and after he had come home and finished dinner he would spend the rest of the daylight hours outside, running around the countryside lost in his own fantasies.

There was only one small difference in his life. The energy of his fantasies had changed. Before, whenever he imagined himself slaying a fearsome beast, it was always the familiar faces from his village that celebrated his achievement. Now, the crowd was bigger.

Hundreds of thousands would surround him from every angle calling his name as he stood at the top of a mountain made of gold.

Instead of conjuring up well crafted statues purely for the joy of creation, he saw himself solving magical conundrums that had puzzled the greatest of minds since the dawn of time. Other Warlocks would congratulate him on his genius telling him how important this discovery was for the future of magic.

At times he wondered if these thoughts indicated that he made the wrong choice in deciding to stay in Hamble. "Not at all," he reassured himself. "This is just my way experiencing Tropolis without having to go there. It's just a phase and it will pass."

One Sunday afternoon, Peter was having lunch with his parents when they heard a quick, rhythmic knocking on the door.

"I'll get it!" said Peter, jumping up from the table.

"Slow down kid. They won't mind waiting a few extra seconds," said his father. But Peter was already gone.

"There's only one person who knocks like that," he thought as he twisted the handle and opened the door.

"Peter!" came a voice from under a thick, bushy moustache.

"Uncle David!" said Peter leaping at him to give him a hug, almost knocking him to the ground.

"It's good to see you Peter," he replied, giving one of his bear-like hugs that Peter loved. "Let me take your bag," said Peter, reaching for it before David could politely refuse.

They stepped inside and went back to the living room. David, exchanged greetings with his sister and brother in law while Peter prepared a few slices of bread and some cheese for his uncle.

"I must say Mary, I need to get out of Tropolis more often. It's a frightfully overwhelming place these days. And it gets more and more intense every day."

Peter almost sliced his finger with the knife when he heard the word Tropolis. He had forgotten his uncle lived there. Strange and uneasy energies began to shift inside him. His mind began to twist and turn with thoughts of adventure. Now going to Tropolis wasn't some huge decision. "I could go with David just for a week," he thought, " Just to see what it's like. Besides it would be good to spend some quality time with my uncle." thought Peter.

"But he said it was overwhelming." thought Peter debating with himself, "Surely that can't be a good thing."

"Perhaps. Perhaps not. But he spends his entire life there. We'll only be there for a few days."

The yearning to see Tropolis with his own eyes had grown in Peter since his conversation with Mr. Silverman. What started as no more than a casual option had slowly matured into a burning desire.

David stayed at the house until the following Saturday. He joined the boys in the field, frequently commending the simple life in Hamble and how stressful living in Tropolis can be. "Don't get me wrong, Tropolis is a wonderful place with everything you could ever ask for. But it does get a bit too much at times."

He certainly enjoyed working the land. "The body needs physical work as much as it does food," he'd say from time to time, "And we just don't get enough of it in the big kingdom." Other times he'd share stories about Tropolis, talking about how the recent advances in magic both amazed and terrified him.

With every story, the fire of curiosity burned hotter and hotter in the heart of Peter. And yet, whenever the thought came to ask David if he would take him to see Tropolis, he avoided it. It wasn't until Saturday afternoon, when David stood at the door with his suitcase and hugged his sister and John goodbye that Peter felt compelled to act.

"David," he asked tentatively, "All your talk about Tropolis has made me curious. Could you take me there sometime?"

David paused for a moment and stroked his chin with his thumb. "Tropolis is an intense place, kid. There's always something to do and you've got to fight a thousand distractions when you want to sit back and relax. Are you sure you can handle it?"

Peter wasn't. There was a nervousness in his stomach and an uncertain voice in the back of mind. "Absolutely!" he declared.

"Then pack your bags, kid. You're coming to Tropolis."

The immediacy of the situation caught Peter off guard. "Now!?" he thought. But there was no time to argue. His body was already halfway up the stairs running to his bedroom.

When his clothes were packed and goodbyes were said, Peter and his uncle began their walk from the farmhouse to the center of the village. Peter had established that he only intended to spend a week in Tropolis, and this allowed him to calm any thoughts of worry that entered his mind.

They passed by Mr. Silverman's House and Peter knocked on his door to let him know he wouldn't be in school for the next few days. "Take this," said Mr. Silverman handing him a sheet of paper, "If you like the big kingdom then meet this man at the academy of Informos. Tell him you're a friend of mine and he'll help you get into any academy in Tropolis." Peter thanked his teacher. But on his way out he reminded himself that he wouldn't need it as once his week in Tropolis was over, he planned to spend the rest of his life in Hamble.

David and Peter walked from Mr. Silverman's house to a nearby wooden barn. In the autumn it would be full of grains and straw for the winter but at this time of year, it was empty. "You'll love this," said David, parting its two large doors.

When Peter saw what was inside, his jaw dropped and his eyes widened. "Wooooaaah!" he said in total awe, "What. Is. That?"

Before them stood a huge creature made of an opal, blue stone. It resembled a human, but its limbs were much thicker and its legs were shorter in proportion to the rest of its body. It stood on all four, perfectly still and beautiful, like one of the sculptures Peter used to dream of making.

"That, my boy, is a speed-golem."

Peter shook his head, grinning in disbelief, "So this is what magic can do." David laughed, "No. This is what magic could do twenty years ago. We've come a long way since then." Attached to the lower ribs of the golem were metal bars that extended behind it, connecting to a shiny metal compartment with a door on either side. "You won't believe how comfortable it is," said David. He wasn't lying. The seats were made of a black, flexible fabric that gently hugged Peter as he leaned back. He closed his eyes and relaxed into the softness, feeling like he was floating in a warm lake that dissolved all the tensions he had accumulated from his morning in the fields.

David entered from the other side. "Check this out," he said and his finger moved to a silver rock that rested in the middle of the compartment. A deep, gravelly voice startled Peter. "Good afternoon, David. How may I help you today?"

"Good day Goliath. Take us to my house in Tropolis. Oh, and my nephew Peter is with us today and I'd like to show him the kingdom from above. Can you take us through the mountains via the twenty seventh southeast road into Tropolis?" There was a brief pause. "The

27th southeast road is under construction. Might I suggest the fourteenth southeast road? The view of the kingdom from Towsen mountain is considered one of top two this side of Tropolis. This route will take twenty seven minutes more than the original."

"Sounds good, Goliath," said David casually.

"Peter sat in disbelief, "Does it really know all that information?"

"That was only the tip of the iceberg. There are one hundred million people in Tropolis, and it knows the address of all of them, and a dozen ways to get to each." David put his finger on the silver rock again. "On we go, Goliath."

"As you wish." The golem let out a loud, hissing noise. Peter watched in amazement as its limbs started to dislocate. The creature quickly took itself apart and reassembled itself in the form of a giant, stone wheel with two metals bars attached to the centre. Then it began to roll. Out the barn. Through the village. And off down an old, dirt road heading north towards the great kingdom. The journey to Tropolis was a silent one. Peter spent the whole trip staring out the window, admiring the countryside as it flashed past him at speed. In his awe, he completely forgot all about his small village, its simple life, and how he would only be in Tropolis for a week.

When they reached the top of Towsen mountain, there was no need for David to tell Peter that this was the view they had come for. In the distance stood a perfect circle, a kingdom surrounded by a huge, stone wall. Buildings rose to the sky and went on as far as the eye could see. The far edge of Tropolis was out of sight. Against a backdrop of a blue sky and a foreground of green and yellow fields, it had a majestic, heavenly quality. "One hundred million," was all he could say.

From the peak of Towsen mountain to the walls of Tropolis, Peter gazed into the distance with anticipation as the magical kingdom came closer and closer. None of his fantasies had ever come close to the reality that approached him and his mind was now frantically updating itself. "One hundred million," he kept repeating to himself.

Peter was still speechless when David opened the door of his dwelling place and welcomed him inside. They had passed thousands of shops and streets, many of which sold wares he hadn't even heard of. David explained every curiosity Peter had asked him but still a thousand more were left unanswered. And David's home was just another sight that expanded Peter's world view to a new dimension of possibility.

Unlike his home in the countryside with its wicker basket, handmade chairs, natural dust and rugged surfaces, David's home was immaculate. Every surface was perfectly clean and polished. The marble counter in the kitchen seemed to radiate light and there was an unnatural stillness that gave the place an air of immortality and permanence.

A yawn escaped Peter's mouth and David realized how tired he must be from his day of travelling. "Let me show you to your room," he said, "We'll have plenty of time to explore the kingdom in the morning."

After seven hours of sleep, most of which was filled with exciting dreams, Peter awoke, feeling refreshed and highly stimulated. He danced into the main room of the apartment. It was a huge room, with a spacious living area on one side, decorated with bright sofas and a padded carpet floor, and a spotlessly clean kitchen on the other, with a perfectly white tile floor, a marble counter and an enormous silver box that Peter had never seen before. "Let's make some bread," he said to David, who was sitting on the sofa sipping a pitch-black beverage. David nearly spat his drink out. "Make some bread? We don't do that here in Tropolis. All our food comes ready prepared. Open that food vault behind you and take whatever you want."

The vault was filled with several dozen foods, half of which Peter didn't recognize. And the ones he did were all in fancy containers. Milk in a clear, thin bottle. Eggs in a rectangle box instead of a basket. The ham was wrapped in a weird, transparent coating similar to the milk. Even deciding what to have for breakfast felt overwhelming compared to the staple bread, eggs and cheese that he used to have back in Hamble. In the end he went for what he felt was an exotic meal; milk and cereal.

The next few days were an endless series of adventure. When David was free, he showed Peter around the kingdom, taking him to food caves, a warrior arena, markets that offered an endless variety of clothes and a thousand shop agorradanium with stalls that offered a magical trinket for every situation you could think of. One night they rode an underground golem that took fifty thousand people half way across Tropolis and they visited a colosseum where two small armies of twenty men battled each other for two hours as Peter, David, and five million others cheered and roared, watching from above.

When David was at work, he arranged for Peter to go on some guided tours and Peter learned about the history of the kingdom, its architecture, its people and its magics.

On Thursday evening, Peter was rummaging through his pockets, when he found the piece of paper Mr. Silverman had given him. "Maybe I should meet this guy before I go," thought Peter, "Just to see what the academy is like. At least then I can tell Mr. Silverman I gave it a look."

When Peter asked David how he could find this man, David took out a small black orb, "I usually don't use this in the house," he told him, "Otherwise, I'd never get a break from work."

"What is it?" asked Peter.

"This, is a black orb of communication. You can use it to speak to anyone else in the world. Provided of course that they have one too."

David asked for a few details about the man and then stared intently into the orb for a few moments. The orb started to sing like a bird and then it spoke in a man's voice, "Hello, Warlock Mendo speaking."

David tossed the orb to Peter who almost fumbled it. "Uh, hello. This is Peter Wheatman. Mr. Silverman said I should speak to you about getting into an academy."

"Silverman? I haven't met that bastard in years. How is he?" The two exchanged a few casual words and agreed to meet up on Saturday at the Informos academy.

The academy was a majestic, incredible blend of architectural brilliance and natural scenery. In the golden afternoon of a cloudless sky young witches and wizards scattered the grounds of the academy. Some were playing a simple game, throwing a strange cylindrical disk to each other as it glided lazily back and forth between them. Others lay casually on the grass engaged in idle chit chat. Others still stood in groups, appearing to be in some sort of trance as they held a mysterious blue orb in their hand.

Peter found Warlock Mendo at a wooden table, outside the academy's tavern. A dark yellow liquid with a frothy white head sat before him in a tall, thick glass. "Warlock Mendo?"

"Ah, you must be Peter," said the man, shaking his hand with a vice-like grip, "It's a pleasure. Take a seat and we'll get you something to drink."

Peter liked Mendo immediately. The conversation flowed naturally and Mendo was quite impressed by the young boy's wit and enthusiasm.

"So," said Mendo midway through their second round of mango fruitbeers, "What branch of magic are you most keen on studying?"

A tricky question. Peter had never had a strong preference for any one subject. He was always the type of kid who became fully engrossed in a subject he had just heard about but would always lose interest after a few days and move on to something new and more exciting.

"I'm not really sure professor. I've always had a strong imagination. And I enjoy seeing things in new and different ways."

"Interesting," said Mendo, stroking his beard, "From our conversation, you give me the impression that you would thrive in the field of blue orb magic."

"What's that, sir?"

"Blue orb magic is one of the most recent areas of magically discovery, and if I dare say so, the future of Tropolis. It's a magic with limitless potential and limitless possibilities. Why, it already runs half the kingdom and it's less than twenty years old."

Peter's heartbeat quicken. "Limitless potential." The thought brought great pleasure to Peter and his mouth began to salivate. This is what he'd dreamed about ever since he was a boy. And now the possibility lay before him. For the rest of the meeting Peter probed and questioned Mendo, posing every question he could think of about these curious blue orbs. "I'd love to answer all your curiosities," said

Mendo looking at his watch, "But I must give a lesson in two minutes on the intricacies of hydropyro magic and its potential in improving golemcraft efficiency."

Mendo got up from the table and began to leave before turning back, "Silverman was right. You'd make a fine addition to our academy. If you do decide to join us. Our next semester starts on the first day of autumn."

On the Sunday afternoon, Peter hugged and said goodbye to his uncle before boarding the steam golem in Southern Tropolis. As the busy streets and meticulous architecture were replaced by green fields and humble trees, Peter reflected on his time in the megakingdom. He couldn't believe that just seven days ago he was working in a field, planting corn with his father and uncle, oblivious to a million different magics that were commonplace just a few hours away. His worldview had been stretched a thousand times over in every direction and thinking about his life in Hamble made him chuckle at how little he knew before. He felt a deep satisfaction, like his journey to Tropolis had shown him everything he needed to know and that if he spent the rest of his life in Hamble, he would never feel like he was missing out. His curiosity had been satisfied and now, there was nothing more that he could even think of wanting.

CHAPTER THREE

First Encounters

It took him more than a week to finish sharing all the wonders he had seen in Tropolis. While his parents were glad that Tropolis had made him happy, they showed no interest in visiting the kingdom themselves. "Good heavens," said his mother when he mentioned his uncle's food vault, "I couldn't imagine not spending my mornings preparing my own bread. I wouldn't let anyone take that away from me."

"It seems a bit excessive," said his father as Peter mentioned the agorradanium with a thousand and one shops, "we only have five shops here in Hamble and they've supplied us with anything we've ever needed."

Peter's adventures in Tropolis had filled him with an unshakable zest for life. He breezed through work in the fields, often planting twenty rows of corn in a single morning. In school his motivation exploded; he posed more questions to Mr. Silverman and joked more with his classmates. His imagination had a new level of intensity, and he jumped from fantasy to fantasy far quicker than he used to. Then something unexpected happened.

One day during breakfast, he surprised himself with the words that came out of his mouth. "Mum. Dad. I'd like to join an academy." They looked at him, a little surprised by his decision and then glanced at each other. "Of course," they said in unison. But before Peter accepted their offer he told them the price, "Warlock Mendo says it will cost four hundred gold coins for the year."

His parents looked at each other again, this time with uncertainty. Four hundred gold coins was several years worth of harvest. They could afford it; they had saved diligently over the years, but it would consume the majority of their life's savings. John broke the silence with a chuckle, "I don't see what else we're going to spend it on." Mary nodded, "We worked hard all these years so that you could have the life you wanted." A wave of gratitude swept over Peter and he jumped from his seat and hugged his parents.

Peter couldn't sleep the night before the first day of autumn. He had spent the past three days in Tropolis, in the accommodation his uncle had helped him find. Tomorrow, every young and aspiring Warlock in the Informos academy would be here for the welcoming ceremony.

Peter had never seen so many people in one place before. Inside the auditorium there were easily seven thousand other students filling the space with excited chatter. Two dozen Warlocks sat on the center stage, dressed in pointy hats and formal robes. Mendo sat among them, relaxed and smiling as he watched over the crowd of this year's initiates. A female Warlock stood up and approached the podium. She was the only one wearing purple robes. She held a black wand with a large bulb at one end to her mouth and moved her lips. "Good morning students." Her voice carried through the entire auditorium and the crowd went silent. A look of awe spread across Peter's face at the marvel of how magic could amplify someone's voice like that.

"I am High Warlock Cecillia Devorious and it is a pleasure to welcome you to the Informos academy of higher magics. This will be a year unlike any other. A year where you will plant the seeds that will bear you fruit for the rest of your life. A year of new friends, new experiences and new discoveries. You are the Warlocks who will shape the future of our beloved Tropolis. And your contributions to magic, will continue to influence our Kingdom for a thousand years to come." A silent energy rippled through the mass of students as they took in the significance of her words.

When the high Warlock had finished speaking, the rest of the two dozen Warlocks took turns at the podium, introducing themselves and the latest discoveries in their field of magic.

Warlock Mistoff, a middle aged man with a brown goatee and sharp facial features introduced himself as the master Warlock of blue orb magic. "...in the past ten years, Tropolis has seen a renaissance in prosperity. The sheer power of blue orb magic has grown beyond anything we could ever have predicted. To those of you who wish to pursue this path, you must take the greatest precautions in making sure that your magic can do as little harm as possible to those who use it. With great power, comes great responsibility."

When the speeches were over, the Warlocks took turns calling for the students who would be studying under them. Peter watched as the auditorium emptied. Then Mistoff took to the podium and Peter and his fellow blue orbers formed a line beside their professor. Peter was surprised by how few in number they were. Out of over seven thousand students, less than forty had chosen to study blue orb magic.

They followed Mistoff out of the auditorium and through an elaborate maze of buildings and pathways. "Don't worry," said Mistoff, "Give it a few weeks and you'll know this place like the back of your hand."

They came to a large rock with twelve entrances, each like the mouth of a cave. They entered the fifth opening which led them into a cold, enclosed space. It was well lit, with a mirror on the back wall that made the space seem far bigger than it actually was. "Take us to the blue orb training cave," declared Mistoff.

"Taking you to blue orb training cave one," replied a voice that reminded Peter of his uncle's speed-golem. He noticed that none of the other students were as impressed as he was at everything around him. The opening of the cave disappeared, and the ground accelerated upwards.

When they stopped moving a huge door opened to reveal a magnificent cave. It was covered with blue, luminous lines that stretched along the walls and the floor and gave the illusion that the room extended on for miles. There were cold, marble seats lined up one after the other and each seat had a large blue orb in front of it. Each orb was as big as a pumpkin and was held secure by a curved, metal bowl that sat on each table. There were four rows of twelve such orbs, and at the end of the cave elevated on a large podium was an orb twice as large as the others.

"Welcome to the future," said Mistoff, as he moved towards the podium at the end of the cave. The students took their seats. Peter gazed into the great, blue orb that sat before him, captivated by the mystique of possibility. The boy beside him laughed, "You never seen a blue orb before?"

"You mean you have?" asked Peter a little embarrassed at his lack of knowledge. The boy laughed again, both shocked and amused that someone wanting to study the most complicated field of magic was so unacquainted with it. "I was raised on blue orbs. We've had half a dozen in my house ever since I was a kid. My parents got me my own "Gremlins World" blue orb when I was seven years old. "

Peter thought back to when he was seven, and how he used to play with wooden figurines he and his father had carved and painted.

"You're not from Tropolis are you?"

"No. Hamble. It's a small village south of here. We don't use magic there." "Don't use magic!?" exclaimed his classmate, "How do you survive?"

Peter told the boy how they make their own bread, farm the land and trade with their neighbours for milk and butter. The boy was equally as fascinated with the simple life Peter had come from as Peter was with the advanced magics of Tropolis. "You're a rare one," said the boy, "I've never met someone so unfamiliar with magic before. Listen, if you don't understand anything about the coursework, just ask me. I built a mini blue orb world over the summer just to see how hard it was. I'm Edvon by the way."

"Peter."

"... ALRIGHTY," declared Mistoff, "Now that you've gotten to know a few of your fellow classmates, let's get a taste of what this course is all about." Everyone turned towards Mistoff. He explained the basics of the course, the schedule they were going to follow, and the standards required of them if they wished to continue studying under him next semester. Finally he reminded them of the power they, as wielders of blue orb magic, possessed and of their responsibility to minimize the risk of harm to those who engaged with their magic. "Now then," said Mistoff, "Let's jump in shall we?" The hairs on the back of Peter's neck stood up. "Today will be a simple lesson. We will enter the blue orb world and manifest a chair."

Peter swallowed. Excitement and worry stirred within him. Suddenly, a wave of dread washed over him, and he felt like he had made a mistake coming back to Tropolis. He didn't have the first idea how to manifest a chair and all of his classmates had years of experience interacting with blue orb magic. "Take your hands and place one on either side of your orb like this," said Mistoff giving a demonstration, "Then focus your mind, intend to enter the orb and..." as he trailed off, Mistoff's body became perfectly still and his eyes glazed over. Peter watched nervously as the rest of the class followed without hesitation. "Don't worry," said Edvon, "It's easy," and with that he placed his hands on his orb and stopped moving. At that moment Peter felt alone. He looked around at the statues that surrounded him, and realized he was the only one still present. "Here I go," he said and he cautiously placed his hands on the blue sphere in front of him. The orb felt cold and it drew out a sigh from Peter as he intended to enter. Suddenly Peter felt a jolt, like he had been catapulted into a distance reality. He felt as if he had become a huge void, a nothingness of endless blue. His physical body had disappeared and all that was left was a formless consciousness.

"Peter is it?" The voice startled him, and Peter imagined turning towards it, though the act of turning didn't quite feel the same in this world. In the endless void, Mistoff stood before him. Though he looked a little younger, taller, more athletic and with a fuller head of hair than the Mistoff from the real world.

"Mendo told me all about you," said Mistoff, "An intelligent boy from a small village that doesn't use magic," Mistoff's words made Peter feel uncomfortable, and he noticed a slight edge in Mistoff's voice. "Blue orb magic is one of the most complicated fields there is. Mendo thinks you're capable enough, but I must let you know that I take my role as master of blue orb magic very seriously, and I won't let anyone become a blue orb Warlock unless they meet the highest of standards. All of your classmates have grown up moving in and out of blue orb worlds, and some of them have already created their own." Mistoff stared directly at the space where Peter felt his consciousness was resting, "Are you sure you're up for the challenge?"

"I...will...do..." Peter struggled to respond to his teacher. While the thought of what he wanted to say came as quickly to him as it normally did, the mechanics of producing sound in this world were foreign to him and the words grated and stumbled against his mind as he tried to produce them. His words slurred and stretched in every direction, and Peter felt uncomfortable, wondering if Mistoff would see this as evidence that he wasn't going to make it through the year, ".. my...best," Peter eeked out the rest of his words. It had taken considerable mental effort to produce such a short sentence. "Let's see how well you manifest a chair," said Mistoff stoically, before giving Peter his instructions. "Imagine a chair in as vivid detail as possible. When you feel that it is fully formed, wrap the chair in a magical coating. This will allow the chair to maintain its form when you relax your focus."

Peter connected to the energetic quality of taking a long, slow, inhale as he focused his mind. He thought back to his parent's kitchen and the wooden chairs that he had sat on a thousand times before. He saw his favourite, with its wicker basket fibers that wove together and the knobbly bump on its left hand armrest. He saw the curved arch that joined each pair of legs and the intricate pattern on the hand knitted cushion that sat on top. When he felt that the chair was as accurate as possible, he initiated the wrapping sequence Mistoff had shown him. "Let's give it a test," said Mistoff, when the wrapping was complete. Mistoff circled the chair inspecting it from every angle. "You've got an eye for detail, at least," he said matter of factly. He stood at the front of the chair and sat down. As soon as he connected with its surface it snapped and Mistoff fell onto the floor.

"Are you all right, sir?" asked Peter nervously.

"Yes, yes," said Mistoff casually, "There's no pain in this world." He stood up, and stared at Peter, "You've picked up speaking in this world, I see." Peter suddenly realized how natural producing words in this world now felt.

"However," said Mistoff, "This chair is unacceptable, and you won't be passing my class unless you fix it. Give it some weight." Mistoff demonstrated to Peter how to unwrap an object. Peter focused his mind again, and tried to imagine how heavy the chair should be. He imagined himself walking up to the chair, sitting in it, picking it up and moving it. When it felt like he had got the weight right, he wrapped it again looking to Mistoff for feedback. As soon as Mistoff looked at the chair he shot towards it. He smashed into the chair head first and Peter watched in horror as his professor's body collapsed in on itself, bones cracking and blood spilling everywhere. Mistoff let out a loud scream as the remains of his body shook violently clinging to the chair. Then he disappeared. A sickly feeling grabbed Peter by the stomach. He'd killed his teacher. And now he was going to be expelled and sent to jail for murder. Then Mistoff reappeared, fully formed and unscratched.

"I'm so sorry," began Peter, but Mistoff brushed him off. "You seem to have set the weight of your chair to a factor of one billion times more dense than it ought to be," he said sternly.

Peter realized that when he was testing the chair, he had imagined the superhuman version of himself lifting it up. The godly version who could split planets in two with a single punch.

"One more time, Peter," said Mistoff, "Our class is about to end." Peter realized that he only had one more chance. He centered his awareness and thought back to the rainy days on the farm, when he lifted the chairs onto the table before sweeping the room. He picked up the chair, flipped it over and rested it upside down on the table. He saw himself rotating the chair and holding it at different angles feeling into how it strained his muscles when he straightened his arms out in front of him. Finally, he wrapped the chair and looked at Mistoff. Mistoff nodded and began the inspection. He circled the chair slowly and then sat down. This time the chair didn't collapse. He rocked slowly from side to side. Then back and forth. He ran his fingers along the wires of the chair and squeezed them. He stood up and gently pushed the chair over watching it fall. He picked it up and lifted it above his head, turning it around several times. Peter felt tense as he watched his teacher examine the chair. It felt like Mistoff was making a list of all the faults and errors in his work. Then Mistoff set the chair down. "Incredible." He turned to Peter, "In all my years I've never seen a chair with so much detail. Most students emphasize all the weight in the centre of the chair or attach it to the ground so that it can't be used for anything other than sitting on. But this... This is something else." The tension Peter was holding onto released and was replaced by a feeling of pride.

Mistoff faced the space that Peter's awareness occupied, "I expect great things from you Peter. Great things."

CHAPTER FOUR

Limitless Potential

*T*he next few weeks were pure bliss. Peter excelled under Mistoff's guidance and he enthusiastically spent hours in the orb cave by himself exploring the boundaries of blue orb realms. He found making new friends quite easy. His handsome face and genuine personality attracted the interest of several women and his honest, happy go lucky worldview made him likeable to the guys. Everyone was fascinated by the boy who grew up without magic. Edvon introduced him to a group of friends and when he tried out for the athletics club, he made the first team of Informos.

Peter had everything he could ever ask for. His life was in perfect balance and there was nothing more that needed to be added...

"This is so easy," thought Peter, with a few scrolls at his side as he began an independent, blue orb study marathon. "All I have to do is show up everyday and do something I love and I'll become the greatest Warlock the world has ever known." He shook his head, dumbfounded at how other students could skip classes and not study in their free time. Last week he had been eating lunch when a group of students next to him admitted they had missed their morning classes and were debating about studying for an exam. "It's not like the material is important," said one. "It's effort," said another lazily.

One Tuesday afternoon, Peter was in an aggoradanium close to the academy, a sixty four story monolith that specialized in selling magical artifacts and paraphernalia for aspiring Warlocks. A butler golem followed Peter around, carrying the food and clothes he had just bought. Peter's mind had been frazzled by two hours of wandering around the agorradanium with its hundreds of millions of items for sale which called and drained on Peter's attention. Now he wanted nothing more than to get back to the simple, green fields on the outskirts of the academy. He was searching for the exit, when the unnatural lure of a blue orb cave awoke his curiosity. The same blue lines of Mistoff's classroom wove into a darkness and Peter felt compelled to enter. "I'll just have a short look around," he told himself, as he stepped inside.

"Good afternoon sir, what can I do for you today?" asked an assistant.

"Well, what do you have?" said Peter, who's confidence with strangers had grown dramatically over the last few weeks. The assistance picked up a rectangular silver card with a battle scene on the cover. There were two Warlocks facing each other, each standing on their own castle as they summoned mythical beasts and golems, cast powerful spells of fire and rallied armies against each other. "This just came out," said the assistant, "Age Of Magiks V," one of the best multiWarlock, blue orb worlds around. Peter was tantalized by the artwork on the cover. This is what his childhood fantasies had been made of and now he had an opportunity to experience it at a whole new level. "You want to give it a try?" asked the assistant. Peter's face lit up, " Yeah!" They walked over to a comfortable seating area and sat down. The assistant handed him a small blue orb that fit comfortably in the palm of his hand. "Call me over if you need anything," said the assistant walking away to give Peter some privacy.

Peter held the orb in his hand gliding his fingers over its smooth, flawless surface. It had the same magical aura as the orbs in Mistoff's cave. Steadying his mind with a focused breath he stared into the orb and squeezed it gently.

He felt the all too familiar feeling of his mind leaving his body and being catapulted to a different reality. But this time, rather than arriving in a voidless space, he landed on solid ground; a muddy cobblestone street bustling with people. "Get out the way," said a tall, angry man as he shouldered through Peter and knocked him to the ground.. Peter felt a rage well up inside him as he got up and prepared to confront him. But the man had already disappeared into the crowd.

"Fresh carrots," came a shrill voice from a stall across the street. "Fresh carrots. Ten for a bronze." Peter followed the voice and saw a haggard old woman with a huge nose covered in warts. She was dressed in dirty clothes and unkempt hair. Peter felt sorry for the woman until he remembered that he was in a virtual world and the woman was no more than a magical enchantment. The rage towards the man who had bumped into him subsided as he took in the detailed environment that surrounded him. The buildings were dirty with cheap, straw roofs, and the people were dressed in a material of such poor quality that even the people of Hamble would have viewed it as primitive.

Then, a deep and soothing voice that felt like it came from all around him spoke. "Ah, the age of alchemy. When humans first learned to harness the power of magic and the might of Warlocks could challenge that of iron and flesh. Where the poverty of the masses first started to dissolve and make way for prosperity. A time of great war and chaos as every Warlock in the land struggled for dominance as they mastered the elements in a bid to gain total power over the world." Then the voice spoke directly to Peter, "Young Warlock, your kingdom needs you to protect them and take them to the land of great abundance. Will you rise to the challenge? Or will you fall at the hands of a Warlock more powerful than thou?"

Peter was enrapt. He wasted no time creating an avatar and running through a simulation that taught him the fundamental mechanics of how this world worked. He launched into a campaign against a Warlock named Hellgamoff and gave everything he could to defend his kingdom. The battle ended quickly. Peter had used all his mana to summon a pack of wolves that would attack his enemy. His opponent who had chosen a more conservative strategy had summoned a dozen farmers to work the lands, and they were helpless to defend themselves against the sharp teeth of Peter's fearsome beasts. As Hellgamoff's simple farmers were torn to shreds the rival Warlock roared obscenities at Peter, calling him a coward for attacking so early. Then he fled the battlefield and the sound of trumpets came from all around him. They played an upbeat melody as an angelic messenger descended from above and cast a spell that made the word "Victorious" shine in bold letters. In a relieved and solemn voice the messenger declared, "The God's of fate look favourably upon you today, young Warlock." The whole spectacle delighted Peter to no end and he eagerly jumped into another campaign. After several victories and a few defeats, he heard a voice that came from the outside world. "How goes the battles, great Warlock?" The words caught Peter just before he entered another campaign and his awareness returned to reality. He sat in the cave as adrenaline, awe and excitement coarsed through his body. "That was brilliant," he beamed at the assistant. "You don't say. You've been in there nearly four hours." Four hours!? Peter hadn't realized how much time had gone by. When he was inside the orb, time ceased to exist. A world of total joy and action. He wanted more.

"How much does it cost?" he asked.

"The world is normally five gold coins by itself," said the assistant, "But we're giving it away for free to anyone who buys the blue orb which is fifty gold coins." His joy vanished. Fifty gold coins was far more than he could afford. He had the money, his parents had given him enough to live comfortably, but the thought of spending so much gold on a luxury such as this made him feel guilty. "I can't afford it," he sighed, slumping into a despondent posture as he came to terms with the fact that his days of smighting Warlocks were over. "That's alright, man," said the assistant, "Tell you what, we don't close for another three hours. You enjoy that world as much as you want until then."

"Thanks," replied Peter, though he was still upset at the eventual end of his adventures in war. Another customer walked in and the store assistant excused himself and left Peter alone. As Peter slumped on the couch he tried to talk himself out of his mood, "It's probably for the best. I could spend all day in this world. I'd never get any studying done."

"Yeah," agreed Peter, though it wasn't doing much to shift his mood, "This was fun but it will probably get boring after a while."

"Boring?" he laughed, "This is the most exciting thing I've ever done. This could never get boring. I could play this all day for the rest of my life and enjoy every minute of it."

"Yeah, well we can't afford it. So let's just play it for the rest of the day and then go home and forget about it."

"Or..." thought Peter whose mind was conjuring up some dangerous thoughts, "We could buy it."

"No."

The part of Peter who always sought to do the right thing awoke fully at the thought of spending the gold his parents had given him for his studies so frivolously.

"But what if we could?" said the part of Peter who yearned to return to the world of battle and victory.

"We can't."

"But it's only fifty gold coins. And besides," said the voice, which has just stumbled upon a thought of juicy persuasiveness, "We aren't just buying this world. We're buying a blue orb. We're going to need one anyways if we want to study over the winter break when we're back in Hamble. This is really an investment in our studies. On top of that, spending time in blue orb worlds like this will help us create better worlds of our own. I've already seen a dozen ways I can improve our work."

"We should go home and sleep on it," said Peter who was feeling uneasy at the effect the world was having on his mind. He knew he wanted to buy the orb solely to engage in magical battles, yet his words were twisted and deceitful, trying to convince himself his intentions were pure. He didn't like his new behaviour yet seemed to willingly allow it. "What's to think about?", said the part of Peter who feared that walking away now could lead to him never fighting another battle, "We need a blue orb for our studies. The world is basically free anyways." Peter watched as the righteous part of him fell silent and this new, deceitful part grabbed the blue orb and marched up to the assistant. "I've changed my mind," he said, with a grin that masked all inner conflict, "I'll take it."

In the weeks that followed the blue orb proved to be a sound investment. The four or five daily hours Peter spent battling ever more powerful Warlocks fueled him with an unrivaled energy. His creativity soared and he raced ahead of his classmates, manifesting ever more complex dynamics inside the worlds he created. It wasn't until Peter lied to his friend that his world began to unravel. Up to the day he bought the blue orb, he couldn't recall a single instance where he had been dishonest. He had no need to, for his conduct and had always been pure.

"Coach is giving us an extra training session this week," said Melissa, one of his teammates from athletics, "Three hours of sprints and acceleration drills. It's going to suck."

"I can't make it," said Peter automatically, "I've got studying to do." A lie. Peter was weeks ahead on his coursework. This was the time he played Age of Magiks and the thought of foregoing exhilarating battles for three hours of mundane training had no appeal to him. A strange guilt washed over Peter. Never in his life had he declined an invitation to engage in physical activity. He'd always loved how good it felt to be in his body, to feel blood coursing through his veins, the joy of his heartbeat pounding against his ribcage and the hard earned sweat dripping from his brough. And yet, now... he felt a slight aversion towards it. The thought of slaying wizards in a fantasy world was so appealing that he lost all interest in a physical workout.

"I have a problem," he admitted to himself as he walked home.

"I need to take a one week break from this game to get my head straight," he said as he opened his front door.

"I'll go to training tonight and run some laps. I'll be glad I did when it's over," he said as he changed into his running clothes and packed some fruit into his bag.

But training wasn't for an hour, and that was all the excuse he needed.

"If I'm not going to enter this world for another week, I might as well have one final goodbye battle before I stop." Peter threw his bag into the corner, grabbed his orb and catapulted himself into the Age of Magiks Universe.

CHAPTER FIVE

Don't Fuck The Witch

*I*t was three in the morning when Peter found himself shaking and short of breath. His eyes were dry and his fingers were stiff. He had been inside the orb for eleven hours, missing both athletic training and an evening get together with Edvon and a few friends.

What just happened? He vaguely remembered telling himself, "Time to go to training," after his second campaign. And responding with an insidious energy, "Training can wait. Just one more battle." One more battle turned into one more battle, and Peter got stuck in a loop that grew harder and harder to break as he engraved the habit of lying to himself onto his mind.

Peter shivered in his bed. This was the first time he had ever not been in control of himself and it scared him. The orb had a strange power over him and could influence his behaviour in ways he didn't understand. When he thought about spending a week outside the world of Age of Magiks, a fearful panic arose within him and he desperately sought out the thrill of another battle .

A rage filled Peter and a scowl spread across his face. He entered the orb and found the magical incantation that wrapped the Age of Magiks world. He focused his energy, broke the wrapping and released the world from his orb. The incantation dissolved in a gentle mist. It was gone. The only way to get it back was to return to the shop and buy the game again and Peter's aversion to spending more of his parent's gold was strong enough to deter him. He was done with this world, and the dangerous lure that it held over him had now been broken...

The next several days were excruciatingly painful. Peter was so accustomed to living inside his orb that readjusting to the real world brought withdrawal symptoms so intense that his friends began to worry. "Are you sure you don't want to see a healer?" asked Edvon, "You look like shit."

"I'm fine. Just a few nights of bad sleep is all." It wasn't exactly a lie. Playing until three in the morning had knocked Peter's sleeping schedule out of rhythm. Not telling his best friend the whole truth felt like he was hiding something. But he reasoned that as long as he went back to living a pure life, there wasn't any benefit to sharing his moment of dishonesty with others. "It'll be easier to forget if less people know," he told himself.

His general mood was depressed, and athletics added another layer of misery. Peter lacked any motivation to engage in training and every sprint was a torture that made him yearn to return to the comfort of his blue orb. He allowed himself the mercy of distracting himself from the pain by replaying magical battles in his mind. He saw no harm in weaning himself off the world with mental fantasies as long as he didn't actually return to the world.

Evenings were the worst. The time he usually spent in Age of Magiks was now an empty void that needed to be filled. He tried to study in Mistoff's cave, but living in a blue orb world made him ache for another battle and he stopped when he found himself flirting with the idea of buying the world again. So when Edvon invited him to a nighttime party in the Mexxon district of Tropolis, he jumped at the opportunity to distract himself from his boredom.

Peter arrived at Edvon's house an hour after dark for the pre party. A group of ten people sat around a table, playing a card game as they consumed various alcoholic beverages.

"Peter my man!" said Edvon as he opened the door and gave him a hug, "Grab a pumpkin beer and join us." Peter synced up with the energy of the room almost immediately. The withdrawals from Age of Magiks had left a residual stimulation that was perfect for socializing. The group laughed and joked and Peter felt his level of excitement rising. When the time was right, a large speed-golem parked outside. "Red flame underground," said Edvon to the driver as everyone squeezed into the back. "You guys want to party, eh?" said the driver playfully.

"Sure do," said one of Edvon's friends and several others started howling in delight. Peter joined in and the group managed to coax the driver into giving them a howl as well. When he did, the group exploded in a cheer and chanted the driver's name over and over, which they read from his name tag. It was a good start to a wild evening.

When they arrived in Mexxon, they joined the end of an eighty person queue. It was Peter's first time in an underground night cave and he was drunk on anticipation. When they reached the entrance two enormous men stood guard. One of them scanned Peter's Tropolis identification card and he eyed Peter for a few seconds before ushering him inside. When Peter entered he was surrounded by total darkness. A strange magic engulfed him, disorienting his senses as he spun around over and over. He stumbled around, feeling dizzy and a little nauseated. He lost all sense of direction and felt like he was falling down, deep into an infinite space. "Edvon," he called out. But no one answered. "Edvon," he called out again. Nothing. His jaw clenched and his eyes rolled up into his head. Realizing he must be under some sort of enchantment he tried to focus himself with sharp, intentional breath.

Slowly, his awareness returned and he could hear loud music. Then the blackness vanished and Peter found himself on an iron platform. "Red Flame Underground," he thought as his eyes lit up at the sight. The cave was filled with a powerful, fast paced music that stirred his soul and enticed him to move. Below was a huge, open space filled with thousands of dancing bodies. A darkness blanketed the cave that was interrupted with flashing beams of red, green, blue and yellow creating waves of light that dissolved in and out of the darkness, like a wild ocean against the shore.

"Yo. How was your trip through the space tunnel?" asked Edvon, who had just entered the cave, "Pretty trippy, huh."

"I thought I was trapped," said Peter, "and I felt really dizzy too."

"That's the point," said Edvon, "They want to disorient your sense of time and space so that when you enter the cave you distance yourself from whatever you were doing before you came here. All your problems are left outside and the only thing that exists right now is this cave. It helps you enjoy the moment more."

"That's insane," said Peter, who had forgotten all about the golem ride here and the party at Edvon's.

"Don't worry," said Edvon, "when you leave this cave it will all come back to you. Now let's go have some fun."

Edvon had reserved one of the tables on the edge of the cave. Here they spent the night switching from dancing to chatting to playing a simple game of dice that involved a little bit of trickery and mischief. Drinks flowed freely and laughter even more.

"I gotta go to the bathroom," said Peter after a particularly riveting game of mokidice. He entered the crowd and slowly danced his way over to the bathroom stalls.

On his way back, as he passed by the seating area in the middle of the cave he felt a strange desire to sit down. As he relaxed into one of the black couches he spread his arms out and let his head hang back.

"Hey handsome," came a voice so smooth and enticing that Peter felt a strong heat flush through him. He turned to the voice and saw a woman. The first thing he noticed was her lips. They were plump and full, with a shiny pink gloss that accentuated their inviting nature. Her brunette hair was thick and curly and it draped down naturally over her naked shoulders. She wore a necklace, a bright green emerald that commanded attention and rested in the centre of her chest. Her large, mature breasts were pushed up, nearly popping out her dress which began slightly above her nipple, and hugged her body tightly, so as to highlight her thin waist and curvy hips. It ended just inches down her thighs, teasing Peter with a glimpse of what lay underneath. The woman held an intense, seductive gaze and Peter felt compelled to return it.

"Hey," he replied, somewhat at a loss for words. He had spoken to attractive girls before but this woman was different. She radiated sexual prowess and every aspect of her body enticed Peter to yearn for her. He felt his breath quicken and an energy stirring in his groin. "I haven't seen you around here before," she said, lightly brushing her fingertips along Peter's arm.

"It's my first time here," he said with a smile that let her know her enjoyed what she was doing, " I'm here with my friends. We have a table over there. You should join us."

"The woman pursed her lips and her face took on a mock hurt appearance, "Don't you want to spend some alone time with me?" she said, with a playful whimper in her voice that ramped up Peter's desire for her.

"I do. I do..."said Peter.

"Oh I knew it. You hate me. You don't find me attractive," she said, pretending to cry and burying her face in her hands.

"No. No. You're gorgeous," said Peter worried that he might have upset her.

"You really think so?" she said, sitting up straight with a surprised smile on her face. "Well in that case..." she leaned over to Peter, letting her plump breast almost brush against his face, as she whispered an incantation in his ear. "If you ever want to see me, just declare that incantation inside a blue orb and you'll be transported into a world of my creation. A world built just for you." She filled her words with a sensual airiness and the image of grabbing her by the hair and kissing her right there flashed across Peter's mind. Peter was surprised by the thought and even more so at how much effort it took to resist acting it out. When she sat back on the couch she smirked at Peter with a playful, knowing look.

"Peter!" came a loud voice from the crowd as Edvon burst into the seating area, interrupting their intimate moment, "We were looking for you man, come join us for another game of mokidice." There was a sense of urgency in his voice and Peter turned to the woman to invite her to join them. He didn't want to say goodbye to her, but when he looked at her she gave him a casual, dismissive look, "Go play with your friends. We can catch up another time." Her words were suggestive and playful. "See ya," said Peter and he followed Edvon into the crowd. As soon as they were a safe distance from the woman, Edvon turned to Peter and grabbed him by the shoulders. "Peter, do you know who she is?"

"No. Why?"

"That woman is a lust witch. They spend their lives mastering the art of sexual magic. Everything about her, her voice, her body, her lip, her tits, is designed to seduce you. She may seem friendly, but her sole intention is to play on your primal desires and make you crave her. If you let her she'll give you so much pleasure, so easily, that you'll lose interest in everything else. Don't fuck the witch, Peter. Promise me, you won't fuck the witch."

"I promise," said Peter with total conviction.

Away from the witch, her enchantment was broken and Edvon's genuine concern showed him how important this was. "I won't fuck the witch." Peter thought about telling Edvon about the incantation she had given him but brushed it aside. It was no big deal. Edvon cracked a smile, "Great. How about another game of mokidice."

Peter enjoyed the rest of the night without so much as an afterthought for the witch. The mokidice and conversation with his friends captivated his full attention and he dwelled in the feeling that all was perfect in this world. It wasn't until he was back in his room, alone and ready to go to sleep that the she returned to him. "Come to me Peter," came her sensual voice. He reached instinctively for the blue orb, but another thought interrupted him. "Don't fuck the witch," warned Edvon. "I won't. I promise," he responded but the promise couldn't restrain his curiosity. "I'm not going to fuck her," he told himself, "But there's no harm in visiting her world. I just want to have a look." He picked up his orb, catapulted himself inside and declared the incantation.

The void around him twisted and danced and he felt himself melting into a different world. Peter arrived in a dark room lit by a dozen candles. A large bed lay behind him padded with a thick, soft duvet and covered in red, heart shaped petals. The air was filled with an intoxicating scent that filled him with desire. The woman from Mexxon stepped out of the darkness. She wore a silky, black corset with a thick, fluffy edge along its border. Her plump breasts had an irresistible appeal to them and away from the crowd of the Red Flame night cave, Peter allowed himself to stare and appreciate them fully. She smiled playfully, "Look as much as you want. It's all yours, handsome." She raised her hands above her head and turned slowly allowing Peter to admire her curves from every angle. Peter felt an erection growing in his pants as his eyes moved from her petite waist to her juicy ass. "Don't fuck the witch," he reminded himself, as she bent over in front of him, revealing the pink flesh the corset had reviously hidden. He swallowed and he felt his dick swell and become rock hard. She stood up, bringing her face just inches from his. "You can do whatever you want to me," she moaned, and a subtle tremor overcame her body, "I exist only for your pleasure."

Peter felt her warm breath on his lips and the way she gazed into his eyes built a mounting tensions within his loins. Peter felt her sensual touch as she rubbed his cock through his jeans. His erection throbbed and he ached for her body. "Don't fuck the witch," he thought, but his words had no strength behind them. "I won't. I only want to see what this world is like." he told himself.

"I'm going to pleasure you all night," said the witch pushing Peter onto the bed. She pulled down his jeans and took his cock in her mouth. Her wet, plump lips wrapped around it, and Peter let out a soft moan as she bobbed her head slowly up and down. "Don't fuck the witch," he told himself. He knew exactly what he was doing. And he knew that if he wanted to stop before it was too late, he had to do it now. He has to get out of the world. The woman let her corset drop and Peter's erection hardened at the sight of her perfect nipples. She cupped her warm, soft tits around his cock and slid them up and down. Peter moaned again allowing himself to fully enjoy the experience. Wave after wave of pleasure followed and Peter lost himself in the heat and ecstasy of the moment. "Do you want to fuck me?" half moaned, half begged the witch.

"DON'T. FUCK. THE. WITCH."

This time the words carried an energy strong enough to break him from his trance. "What am I doing?" he asked himself, and for instance the witch's enchantment weakened its grasp. "I made a promise that I wouldn't do this." In that moment, he was fully ready to leave the witch and return to the real world without breaking his oath.

But he hesitated. And in that moment of indecision, the witch's magic whispered seductively in his ear, "It's okay. I'll only fuck her once. Just for the experience. After tonight, I'll leave this world and never come back." And Peter, with every fibre in his body yearning for the pleasure of the witch pulled her onto the bed and fucked her.

CHAPTER SIX

Drop By Drop

With a loud moan of pleasure, Peter ejaculated inside the witch. An orgasm rocked his loins and a chorus of blissful sighs escaped his lips. "That was incredible," he said, rolling onto his back. The woman rolled onto her side and carressed Peter's chest. "You can come back anytime," she said, resting her head on his shoulder. Edvon's words came back to Peter, "Don't fuck the witch." He could see his friend shaking his head in disappointment knowing that he had broken his trust. But as he lay on the bed, with a beautiful woman in his arms, he wondered if his friend had been overly cautious. "After all," he reasoned, "That felt amazing. What's wrong with enjoying myself once in a while." Peter lay with the woman for some time before he remembered he was in a blue orb world. "My physical body must be feeling tired right now," he thought. After saying goodbye to the woman, he focused his mind and catapulted himself back to his bedroom. When he arrived he was caught by surprise. He was sitting in his chair, with a blue orb in his right hand and his limp penis in the other. His trousers were around his ankles and semen covered his left hand and thighs. He laughed. "So that's why it felt so real."

When he played Age of Magiks or studied in Mistoff's cave, it was always clear that his physical body was in a different location to his awareness. But inside the witch's realm he thought he could feel her touch. "So she wasn't real at all?" he thought, "Or at least no more real than the Warlocks in Age of Magiks." He shrugged. He didn't really care. All he knew was that it felt incredible and that he could visit that world anytime he wanted. "Edvon was overreacting," he told himself, "There's nothing wrong with fucking a witch every now and again."

Just like with Age of Magiks the next few weeks felt like a renaissance to Peter. Basking in the pleasures of the lust witch every night made him feel like a king. And as he only spent an hour or two with her, far less than the four or five that Age of Magiks consumed, he had more time to invest in his studies. Life was back to where it should be. Until it wasn't.

It started with athletics. His drive to give his all to every single sprint dampened and he felt a subtle lack of strength in all his movements. His studies followed. Three hour marathons of exploring the limits of blue orb magic no longer appealed to him. A night of pleasure with the lust witch awaited him no matter how much work he completed. But after a few weeks with the witch, her appeal waned and Peter saw with more clarity what his visits were costing him.

Her enchantment was losing its power and had she stood alone against Peter in the battle for his time and energy, Peter would have broken her magic and regained his freedom. In his time with her, Peter had realized that the woman he visited every night was not the same one from the Mexxon night cave. Rather, she was a virtual avatar, a magical conjuration that replicated her physical body and a few dozen routine action sequences the woman had performed once and then wrapped in a magical coating, for infinite reuse. The woman he slept with was no more real than the endless minotaurs and fire bolts he summoned in Age of Magiks.

One day, when the witch's spell no longer enticed him and a boredom for her routine movements was setting in, a curiosity overtook him. Peter went searching and found something more powerful than he could ever have dreamed of.

A megaworld. A world of worlds that Peter could access with a single incantation. When he entered the world he stood before by a thousand doors and when he opened one, fifty lust witches surrounded him surrendering themselves to his will. Each witch held a blue orb that would take Peter to a private world.

Peter felt like a God. All these witches wanted him, craved him, yearned for him and Peter took a twisted satisfaction in knowing they were all competing for his time and attention. He had all the power. A thousand women waited on him, existing solely for his pleasure. In less than a month after Mexxon, Peter had fucked over a thousand witches and showed no desire to slow down. Of course, he didn't fuck them for an hour each, like he had the first witch. How could he? And why would he devote so much time to a single woman when so many others craved his cock? His new pattern involved entering a room of fifty witches, choosing one, taking her stone and going to her world, thrusting inside her a few times in several different positions, and then quickly returning to the room full of witches, where a fresh and novel body waited for him. In this manner, he'd regularly fuck one hundred or more witches in a single night, in marathon sessions that stretched well beyond his previous two hour limit. His hedonic assemblies always ended with Peter catapulting himself back to reality, finding himself alone in his room gripping his limp cock with semen covered fingers. Reality always filled him with a feeling of regret, but the overwhelming pleasure he gained from the witches drowned out the discomfort.

One night at a house party Peter finally realized how much he had changed. Edvon threw a large party to celebrate the completion of a particularly hard week of academic tests. Peter was chatting to a girl in the kitchen and his attraction for her was mounting. His daily habit of chronic lust witch encounters had rewired his mind to look for sexual activity everywhere.

The girl was rather confident and flirty and had touched Peter's arm several times while gazing into his eyes. Just one month ago, Peter would have seen this as an invitation to kiss her, like anyone normal person who hasn't rewired their minds with a thousand warped, sexual encounters, with avatars whose sole purpose is to satisfy your sexual desires.

Avatars who must offer increasingly novel and taboo sexual activities so as to out compete the ten thousand other witches struggling for your attention. So when the girl played with her hair and gently bit her lip, Peter's warped mind saw it as a declaration that she existed solely for his pleasure and would fulfill any desire he requested. Peter grabbed her hand, "Let's go upstairs. There's a free bathroom we can use." She yanked her hand away, "What the fuck is wrong with you?" she shouted, her pretty face distorting into a scowl. "You think I'm going to fuck you on the toilet?" Peter's face flushed with embarrassment, "It was a joke..." he said laughing nervously. "Sure," she said, shaking her head in disgust and walking away before Peter could respond. She joined her group of friends and Peter knew she would tell them what he had done. He felt sick and sat down on the staircase debating over what to do. "I could deny it," he thought but it didn't feel like a good idea. He didn't feel comfortable trying to convince everyone that she was a liar, and the uncertainty that he could've done it would hang over his reputation forever.

"Hey, Peter. Are you okay?" It was Melissa from athletics.

"Not really," said Peter, "I made a really stupid joke and now I feel like an asshole."

"Aww it can't have been that bad. What did you say?"

"I took a girl's hand and told her to come to the bathroom with me. But I think I was too convincing and she thought I was serious."

"Well... it's not your best joke," said Melissa sympathetically," But you shouldn't feel like an asshole about it. I know you Peter and you're not that type of guy."

"Do you?" he thought. She knew the old Peter. The respectful, honest and hardworking Peter who hadn't spent the last four weeks visiting ever more extreme and deviant lust witch worlds. He'd managed to keep his social and his private personalities separate until a few moments ago, when they first started to merge. The realization of his transformation depressed him, but right now he had a reputation to protect.

"Yeah, I guess you're right," he said, "It was just a joke."

"Come on, where is she?" said Melissa, "I'll go and explain to her that it was just a joke and you're not like that." Peter pointed her out and they walked over. Melissa did most of the talking, arguing feverishly on Peter's behalf. When she finished the girl reluctantly agreed to take Melissa's word for it, but any chance of a romantic relationship was dead. As they walked away, Peter felt intense gratitude for Melissa. But he knew this was a wake up call. He knew that he needed to permanently cut lust witches out of his life and seriously reevaluate who he wanted to be.

CHAPTER SEVEN

The Devil's Snare

*P*eter left the party early and walked home alone. He replayed the interaction over and over in his mind wondering how much of the interaction was actually his fault. "Was I really that bad?" he wondered, "No. That bitch was a prude. Any other girl would have been thrilled to be fucked in the bathroom." When he heard his own thoughts it disgusted him.

"Look at me. How am I even thinking this? I'd never have done this a few months ago. What's happened to me?"

"People change," he said, "And besides, I'm a man. It's natural for me to want sex." He was half right. The drive to procreate was hardwired into his body. But the natural drives had been warped and engrossed by excessive encounters with lust witches. A few weeks ago, he could spend an hour lying in bed with a single woman enjoying every moment. Now, he couldn't fuck a witch for more than a minute without growong bored and seeking out a novel playmate. His tastes had warped too. Regular sex no longer appealed to him and fucking witches who would roleplay as his mother or sister became normalized. Walking up to a witch on a busy street and fucking her infront of a thousand passerbys had become routine. Sometimes, a single witch lacked the attractiveness to arouse him and two, three or even ten were needed to give him an erection. Had he known what he would become, when he first met the witch that night in Mexxon, he never would have entered her world. But her sexual magic pulled him in with the promise of ecstasy, and once he was in her cauldron she slowly turned up the heat in such small increments that he allowed himself to be a willing accomplice in his own tragic decline. He had fucked the witch. And paid with his character.

When he was back in his room the first thing he did was reach for his orb. The sting of rejection from the girl hurt more than he liked to admit, and the unconditional devotion of the witches was a soothing balm that could temporarily distract him from reality. He entered the world and lost himself in bitter pleasure.

"What the fuck did I just do?" gasped Peter, horrified at the state he found himself in. The sun was rising when Peter returned from an eight hour lust witch binge. There was semen on his hand and legs and in the shiny, perfect surface of his blue orb, Peter saw the reflection of a drained and broken man. "This has to stop," he said, a panic in his voice, a natural response to the vivid clarity he now saw himself with. Regret, shame, disgust and guilt poured into him as he realized the damage he had done. "I have a problem," he admitted, "A serious problem."

The following week felt like a nightmare. Without the daily release of easy pleasure chemicals, Peter lost all motivation to do anything and his energy levels plummeted. It became a battle to get out of bed in the morning and Peter skipped athletics training and class with Mistoff. When he noticed his cravings for "Just one more visit," to the lust witches growing out of control, he created a complex guardian enchantment inside his blue orb that required intense mental effort to remove. The guardian was commanded not to allow Peter to visit any lust witches and it proved incredibly effective on the several occasions that Peter's will broke and he desperately searched for his familiar poison. To distract himself from the intense withdrawals, Peter went for long walks by the river that flowed through the forest on the edge of the academy.

The time in nature reminded him of home and Peter found himself at the base of a large, oak tree weeping.

"What have I done?" he asked thinking back to how innocent and honest he was just a few months before, "This isn't who I want to be."

He thought about his parents, how ashamed they'd be if they knew what he had done. How hard they worked their whole lives and how he spent their gold on a blue orb that brought him nothing but self destruction. "I've got to stop this," he told himself, "how did I let things get so bad?"

As he searched the archives of his mind he realized there was no single moment where everything fell apart. His fall from grace has been a gradual process, a little more lewdity here, one extra lust witch than the night before there. Drop by drop, he had whittled away at his character as he surrendered to his base pleasures and became a slave to his lust. The witches didn't serve him. He served them. With every thrust and lustful gaze he offered them his energy and power. He traded his ability to enjoy lying with a single woman, for the pleasure of fucking a thousand witches in a single night. Every visit brought less and less enjoyment until the entire megaworld harem could no longer satisfy him. He was chasing the enjoyment he felt on his first night with a witch, and deep down he knew he'd never relive it by pursuing pleasure. "I've got to stop,"he told himself, "I've got to get my self respect back." It took a week of abstinence before Peter felt better. He wasn't fully recovered but he was strong enough to go to athletics and Mistoff's cave. He told his teacher and his coach that he was sick with food poisoning. They didn't need to know the truth. No one did. All that mattered was that Peter stayed clean.

For three weeks Peter lived a pure and honest life. He abstained from even thinking about the lust witches and immediately shut down any thoughts of returning to their realms. He started doing three hour study sessions again and although they weren't as satisfying as they used to be, Peter persisted with them. "I've overwhelmed my pleasure centres with supernatural levels of pleasure," he told himself, "It's going to take some time before I'm back to normal." When the winter exams came around, Peter breezed through them. He scored top marks in every area and it helped to restore a certain level of pride. "I'm back," he said, "I've beaten the witches."

Peter had planned to spend the three days after the exams at the academy before returning home to Hamble for the winter. His final exam had finished at midday and he was free until eight that evening, when he would meet his friends. Sitting on his bed, thinking about how good it would feel to return to his village, he suddenly remembered a conversation he had heard a few weeks ago. He was on his way to Mistoff's cave, when he overheard two students talking about a new , free-to-enter blue world called League of Warlocks. Their enthusiasm has sparked a curiosity in Peter, but he refused to pursue it, as he knew how easy it would be for the world to consume all of his time. But now was different. He had a party to go to in seven hours and he would return to Hamble in three days. Outside circumstances limited the amount of time he could spend in the world, even if he did lose track of time. "Besides," he told himself, "I earned it. I worked really hard these past few weeks and deserve some fun time." He grabbed his orb, declared the incantation and catapulted himself into the world.

Peter landed in a sparsely furnished room. A sturdy, oak table was positioned in the centre and he and four other Warlocks stood around it. An intricately detailed, three dimensional map of a battlefield was projected onto the table. A voice from above spoke, "Warlocks, you have been summoned here because you have shown exceptional ability in the art of combat. The enemy team has five Warlocks of equal caliber. Your objective is to destroy their base before they destroy yours. Please choose your weapons and artifacts wisely. The battle will begin in ninety seconds." Peter felt the familiar excitement of combat charging up inside him. It had been too long since he'd had a good battle.

"We need a shield master," said one of the other Warlocks. "Who here can play the role?"

"What's a shield master?" ask Peter.

"Oh, God. He's never played before," said another Warlock, "Looks like we're the underdogs."

"A shield master is someone who protects the rest of the team," said the first Warlock, "They can take more damage than any other Warlock, but they also deal less damage than everyone else."

"Got it," Peter said.

"If it's your first time playing, you should be a shield master," said a third Warlock, "With their health and defense perks, you can make more mistakes and won't be punished as badly."

"Okay, I'll be a shield master," said Peter.

"Just listen to what I say and you'll do fine," said the first Warlock," I've got a lot of experience playing shield master so I can teach you what to do."

"The battle will begin in ten seconds," declared the voice, and Peter and his teammates selected their weapons and artifacts before the world filled with light and they were transported to their base.

Peter liked this world already. The pre battle conference had filled him with a sense of comradery that Age of Magiks lacked. Now he wasn't fighting for himself. He was fighting for the team. Peter looked around his base. A giant stone tower stood in the middle with a huge red crystal at the top. The ground was covered in old, ruined stones with clumps of grass in between them. His allies wore various outfits, one was dressed in a Warlock's robes, another in the chain mail armour of a knight. Everything looked so real. "The enemy has entered the battlefield," declared an omnipotent voice that snapped Peter into awareness. "With me, Peter," said a Warlock who carried a bow and arrow, and Peter followed him out the eastside entrance of their base.

Peter was a natural shield master. With his teammate's guidance he quickly mastered the basics of when to attack, when to retreat and how to work with his teammates for maximum efficiency. The game ended with Peter and his allies bombarding the enemy tower to the ground with a barrage of magical and physical assaults. "Victory!" declared the omnipresent voice, as the red crystal shattered and the great stone tower crumbled to the ground. A ball of light surrounded each of the five Warlocks and they were transported back to the room with the sturdy, oak table.

"That was incredible," said Peter to his new allies.

"You did really good," said the Warlock who had doubted him.

"Who's up for another battle?" said Peter who had tasted the sweet nectar of victory and wanted more. Then he remembered that he had to go to a party at eight and felt disappointed that he would have to stop playing eventually. "Better make the most of it," he told himself, as he and his comrades were teleported to a new battlefield.

One more battle led to another, and at ten to eight, Peter decided that he could fight just one more before going to the party. It would make him a little late, but no one would really care.

The battle lasted longer than he had expected. His opponents were skillful warriors and Peter and his comrades fought valiantly for forty minutes before finally conceding defeat. "I should probably go to the party now," said Peter, but the thought of leaving after a loss bothered him. "Just one more," he told himself, "I'm already late and another battle won't be the end of the world." Another battle turned in four, as Peter hit a string of defeats before finally securing a victory. When the battle ended it was twenty past ten and Peter had to stop himself from automatically jumping into another battle. "Fuck," said Peter realizing how late he was. He paused considering fighting just one more battle before finally pulling himself away from his orb and out the house.

"Sorry I'm late," he told his friends when he arrived, "I took a nap and only just woke up."

For the whole night Peter's attention was divided. While he enjoyed the relaxed atmosphere and company of his friends, his mind was preoccupied with new strategies and tactics he wanted to test out in League of Warlocks. He managed to stay until the end of the party, when some of his friends who were leaving early said their final goodbyes before the winter break. "I'll miss you, Peter," one of them said to him. "I'll miss you too," said Peter and he meant it. But he didn't feel it fully. They had a great friendship but the excitement of League of Warlocks overshadowed his real life and he could easily spend a month in that world without a second thought about any of his friends. Naturally, when he returned to his bedroom he immediately reached for his orb. Sleep could wait. All he wanted was to get back to his favourite world.

Five days later, Peter finally put down his blue orb. A massive headache racked his skull and his fingers were stiff from holding the orb. His eyes were dry and strained and a sluggish energy saturated his body. "Damn," thought Peter. His blue orb battles had been a thrilling adventure but he knew he had overdone it. He had missed two days of goodbye parties with his friends and was another two days late on his plans to return to Hamble. He stared at the orb, stroking it and contemplating whether he should fight another battle or pack for Hamble. He chose packing and as he filled his bag with clothes and some exotic foods he had bought as a gift for his parents, he debated over bringing the blue orb back to Hamble. "I could get some serious study done over the winter," he told himself, but he knew better. The thought of his parents seeing him spend all day inside a blue orb while he played League of Warlocks was enough to deter him from bringing the orb home.

Peter took a rail golem to a town thirty thousand paces east of Hamble. It was the closest station to his home and a horse and cart took him the rest of the way. Peter dreaded seeing his parents again. He felt that as soon as they saw him, they would know just by looking at his face, all the deviant things that he had done. But when he opened the kitchen door, he was greeted by nothing but open arms and unconditional love. All the lies, dishonesty, lust witches and warped thinking vanished and he became his old self again.

"I missed you," said his mother, giving him a hug.

"There's my boy," said his dad wrapping his arms around the two of them. When they asked about Tropolis, only the memories of good friends, Mistoff's cave and the wonders of magic came to him. He eagerly shared stories about all the wonderful magics that Tropolis held and how advanced blue orb magic had become.

A few days after he arrived, Peter began to notice some changes within himself. When he made bread or chopped wood with his parents he enjoyed it thoroughly, but when he was alone, he felt a slight aversion to doing any physical work. "Effort," he thought lazily one day, when he had chopped enough wood for the evening and thought about chopping enough for the rest of the week. He remembered how in Age of Magiks he could summon a farmer who would chop wood continuously for him without a second thought. "Why can't reality be that easy," he sighed, putting the axe down and carrying the logs inside.

On the rail golem back to Informos Peter realized how little he had thought about Tropolis or blue orb worlds during his stay in Hamble. "That was all I needed," he told himself, feeling proud about his total lack of desire for lust witches or Warlock battles, "My time on the farm has renewed my strength and given me some much needed clarity."

It wasn't until he was back in his room, alone and tired from a day's travel, with his blue orb within reach that the desires returned. "I suppose one round of League of Warlocks couldn't hurt," he told himself, "I'm stronger now, I can stop after one round." He catapulted himself into his blue orb and all the thrills and excitement of battling Warlocks with his comrades returned.

"All right," he told himself, when the battle was won, "Time to put this away and unpack."

Peter was surprised by how easy it was for him to leave the blue orb world. As he unpacked his bags and put his clothes away he felt a strong sense of confidence. "I've beaten my addiction," he told himself, "I can stop at anytime." He was so happy with himself that as soon as he finished unpacking he rewarded himself with another visit to the League of Warlocks realm. But this time, after the battle was won, he stated another. And another. Then a sadness came as he realized how his cravings to keep playing were returning. He knew that this was a pivotal moment in his life.

"I'm not as strong as I thought I was," he admitted to himself putting the orb down. He sat on his bed and thought about his life and how his actions today would dramatically affect his future. "I can keep fighting battles right now and spend half of the semester inside that world," he thought, "Or I can accept that I can't play this game in moderation and spend the rest of my life in the real world." He weighed the two options against each other. A normal, healthy life full of friends and athletics, hard work and study, living with honour and experiencing reality in its fullness.

Or a supernatural life. Full of Warlocks and heros, epic battles that transcended time and the comradery of four other Warlocks who fought beside him.; the chance to become the most powerful Warlock who ever lived, in a fantasy world that seemed more real than life. Sure, if he chose this path there would be times where he would leave the orb with stiffened fingers and a groggy feeling caused by two days without sleep, but such was the price for the glory of war. As he weighed up the two options Peter felt divided. He knew in his heart that the healthy, normal life was the right path for him to take. The blue orb had an unnatural power over him that caused him to value fighting another battle more than food or sleep, more than his health and even his friends. And yet he felt drawn to the path. Like a moth that flies into a candlefire even though it knows it will be scorched. "I really shouldn't do this," he told himself and he wrapped his fingers around his orb and lost himself inside.

CHAPTER EIGHT

Hesitate And A Decade Passes

*T*he next seven years were not particularly favourable for Peter. While his natural genius allowed him to complete his training as a blue orb master, he never pursued his childhood dream of becoming the world's greatest Warlock.

The world of League consumed him and he would spend months at a time fighting battles in a magical world, his awareness disconnected from reality. Occasionally he would break these cycles by refusing to enter the world and get his life together but his attempts never lasted more than a few weeks. Leaving the blue orb world brought his attention back to his body, and as it slowly returned, he became more and more aware of a pain inside him.

Perhaps it was the residual effect that months of poor posture, lack of movement and poor sleep unavoidably bring or perhaps it was the pain of realizing he had wasted years avoiding life and that he had missed out on moments he could never get back.

Perhaps it was the pain of isolation, of slowly distancing himself from his friends and family because he dreaded the thought of them showing a genuine interest in his life and having to hide how he really spent his time.

Or perhaps it was the pain that naturally results from lying to yourself that you will quit and then watching helplessly as you continue to engage in the same behaviour over and over, a pain that he could avoid feeling by escaping into the world of League.

It wasn't just League of Warlocks that consumed Peter. One night he was overcome with lust and managed to overcome the guardian enchantment and return to the world of pleasure.

From then on lust witches became a regular part of his life and he made and broke vows to never return to them just as often as he did with League.

One morning, deep into a three day binge of fucking witches and killing Warlocks, his orb broke. Peter and his team were on the verge of tearing down the enemy tower when he found himself catapulted back to his room.

"No! No!" He shouted, squeezing his orb as he desperately tried to return. A panic attack followed and Peter was like a trapped animal trying to claw his way back into the safety of his orb. When his fear subsided and his awareness returned to the room he was in, he spoke the words he had said a thousand times before, "I need to stop this. Why can't I stop?"

Peter broke down and sobbed. He didn't understand. He didn't understand why he was so powerless over his own actions. He didn't understand why he compulsively entered a world that corroded his health and character with every visit. He didn't understand why he would rather stay in a world that he vowed to leave, that he knew was destroying him, instead of living life in the real world. He thought back to how strong, joyful, wholesome and honest he used to be, and didn't understand why he would willingly trade it all away for some short lived gratification.

The orb had taken everything from him. His mental faculties had dulled. His motivation to feel alive had been sapped away so that only the drive to enter the blue world remained. His health had declined as he sacrificed food, sleep and movement to remain inside the orb. He walked into his bathroom and looked in the mirror. A zombie looked back at him. Bloodshot eyes with heavy, black bags under them, eyes that had lost their spark for life long ago. Dirty, unwashed hair and sickly, pale skin. "I've got to stop," he told himself again, but there was no energy in his voice. He spoke with a total apathy that mirrored his internal state. He'd said these words a thousand times before and every time he'd failed to follow through.

But now things were different. His orb had burned out. He couldn't return to the supernatural worlds even if he wanted to. This was his one opportunity to turn things around. He knew that if he didn't take major action right now he would eventually buy another orb. He could see himself in the agorradanium, walking towards the blue orb cave, knowing that he was destroying his life and refusing to stop himself as he watched himself buy another blue orb. If that happened, he wouldn't get another chance. It would be suicide. Killing himself by refusing to live in the real world, by willingly confining himself to the dimensions of a small blue stone. He couldn't let that happen.

The awareness of the pain inside his body slowly increased and Peter wanted to bury his head in a pillow until he fell asleep. But this wasn't the time for more procrastination. Barely able to stay awake, he dressed himself and went outside.

As he walked the street, people stared and took extra care to avoid bumping into him. He hadn't showered in weeks and looked sickly and unkept.

"What the fuck is wrong with me?" he asked himself. At eighteen his life was perfect, his future was a promise of unlimited potential. At twenty five he had blossomed into a pathetic mess. A sack of energetic knots of addiction, agony and wasted potential.

Peter didn't know where he was going. His mind had been numbed by over thirty hours without sleep. He stumbled about in a daze, going nowhere as he fought his urge to collapse on the street from exhaustion.

CHAPTER NINE

The Source Of Self Destruction

*P*eter didn't know how long he wandered the streets of Tropolis before stumbling upon a small sign in a shop window.

"Hex Removal. Master Warlock with three decades of experience will remove any hex that has been placed upon you."

The words brought a sudden realization, "That's it. I've been cursed. That's why I couldn't control myself. That's why I couldn't stop." A hopeful excitement filled him and he pushed through the door and marched inside.

Inside the building a lady sat behind a large marble counter. "I need a hex removal," said Peter rather bluntly. She eyed him up and down, "You sure do, honey. Do you have an appointment?"

Peter shook his head. "Let me check our schedule," she said and gripped a small blue orb that rested in a silver bowl on the edge of her desk. She froze for a second, and then with a sigh regained her ability to move. "Warlock Gregory has a free slot in two hours."

"I'll take it," said Peter.

Peter found a row of seats where he could wait for his appointment. Initially he battled to stay awake, drifting in and out of consciousness, but he eventually succumbed to the needs of his body and fell asleep.

"Sir," said a voice as a hand gentle shook him awake, "It's time for your appointment."

Groggy and barely conscious, Peter got up and followed the lady to the Warlock's office. She let him in, wished him good luck and closed the door behind him.

Inside the room was a leather black couch and a wooden chair. A man who was standing by the window looking out over the kingdom turned and greeted Peter. "You're here for a hex removal, I take it. Rest assured, I've removed over five thousand hexes in this office and I'll be able to remove yours too. Tell me, what seems to be the issue?"

The man had a short white beard and his face possessed a youthful glow. He spoke with a jolly tone, earned through decades of success, an example of how his clients will feel when their hex is removed.

"I have a problem," said Peter. The Warlock motioned to the black sofa and Peter took a seat. The man had a kindness to him that made Peter feel safe enough to open up about his shameful past. This was the first time Peter allowed himself to speak of his actions to another human.

He shared how perfect his life used to be back in Hamble, how gifted he was, how much potential he had and how much of a failure he felt for not living up to it. He told him about League of Warlocks and the lust witches, how fighting another battle became more important than food or sleep or going to his friend's birthday. He told him how warped his sexual tastes had become and how he continued to visit the lust witches long after he received any enjoyment from their company. He shared the moment at the party when he invited a girl to fuck him in the bathroom and how he started seeing women as nothing more than objects that he could use to satisfy his sexual impulses. He shared his decline, from a man bound by honour, health and honesty to someone weak and shameful, desperate for immediate satisfaction. He told him how many times he'd lied to himself, that he would stop League and lust witches and start living an honest life, and how he always returned to his vices. "I just want my old self back," he admitted, as he weeped uncontrollably. Warlock Gregory listened with total attention and compassion. He took in every word Peter spoke, and comforted him with gentle words.

"My boy," he said, placing a hand on his shoulder, "You've been through a lot." His voice soothed Peter, in a natural and healing way that another battle in League of Warlocks never could, "But you have not been hexed." Peter stopped crying and looked up at the Warlock.

He was confused. "A hex is a very complex magical conjuration. It takes a skilled Warlock intense effort to produce."

"Then why did I do all these things to myself?" sobbed Peter. The Warlock could feel the anger and confusion in Peter's voice, "Because you are human," he told Peter, "And we were never built for the abundant world we now live in. For millions of years, we lived in a world which lacked any of the advanced magics that are commonplace in Tropolis. A world where you had to spend all day foraging just to feed yourself. You'd be lucky if you slept with a single woman in your entire lifetime. Now you can enter your orb and a thousand women are lining up begging for your seed. This is not an easy offer to refuse when your body is conditioned to make reproduction a top priority." As Peter listened he thought back to how happy he was with his simple life in Hamble and how the supernatural abundance of Tropolis had subtly enticed him with its irresistible enchantments. The hypernormal pleasures of a blue orb gave him more stimulation in a single day than most of the villagers in Hamble had experienced in a lifetime. "Your brain is wired for scarcity," continued Gregory, "And it believes that the thousands of lust witches that offer themselves to you today could be gone tomorrow and that now you must seize the opportunity before it vanishes. Your problem wasn't being hexed by an evil curse, but being drowned in an excess of abundance. There is nothing wrong with devoting all your energy to a rare pleasure that is naturally fleeting, but when the same pleasure has been immortalized through supernatural enchantments, the same indulgence will destroy you. You didn't fuck a thousand witches. You fucked one witch at a time, expecting the abundance to end in a world that knows no scarcity. You became stuck in a world of pleasure that never ends."

"I don't want to be stuck in this world," said Peter, "I want my old self back."

The Warlock shook his head. "No you don't. You want lust witches and epic battles. That's why you keep going back. You might think you want your old self back, but you want these pleasures more. That's why you chase them." Peter felt angry. How dare this man tell him that he wanted to remain trapped in a life that brought him nothing but misery and pain. He wanted to defend himself. But he wasn't here to argue with the Warlock. He was here to overcome his addictions. "How can I get my old self back?" he asked.

"You can never fully return to who you were," said the Warlock, "All actions have consequences and you've spent seven years living in the land of instant gratification, wiring your mind to seek out easy pleasures." Peter's heart sank, "So there's no hope of recovery?" "I didn't say that. You can recover. You can even build a better life than the one before. Give it a few years and you'll feel like your old self again." A few years was a long time and Peter wondered if he had the strength to abstain from blue orbs for so long. "But," said Gregory, looking Peter directly in the eye, "You can never let your guard down. You've created a dangerous circuit in your brain, and a single visit to a lust witch or the world of League of Warlocks will reawaken it and drag you right back down to where you are in this moment. Your journey home begins now. If you want your old self back, you can never visit a blue orb world again." Peter knew these words were true. He recalled all the times he told himself that he would fight "Just one more battle," and two days later he was still inside his orb. He thought back to his life before Tropolis and how every moment felt like a gift. He needed nothing, wanted nothing. Life was whole and complete. He knew that returning to this state was the greatest gift he could give to himself. And yet, the thought of giving up League and the witches felt uncomfortable. It cast a shadow of meaninglessness over his life and his future seemed empty without them.

"I don't know if I can," admitted Peter, "I've promised myself a million times before and broke them all."

"It won't be easy," said Gregory, "But ultimately it's up to you to quit. Whether you fail or succeed, you're the one who will have to live with the consequences of your actions for the rest of your life. The next few weeks will be hard. Your body will crave blue orbs as it readjusts to a life without constant stimulation."

"And then I'll feel better?" asked Peter hopefully. Gregory let out a chuckle and shook his head. "Then you'll feel more. There is an immense pain within you waiting to be felt. Eventually it will rise to the surface of your awareness and you will have a choice to make. In the uncomfortable pain and boredom, you can choose to sit still and listen to your pain, or you can numb yourself by returning to the pleasures of a blue orb. This won't make the pain go away. It wi' merely bury it even deeper inside you. The choice to feel it or flee from it will be yours when the time comes."

"I don't know if I can," admitted Peter.

"I don't know either," said the Warlock and a long silence followed. Eventually Peter spoke, "What should I do?"

Gregory thought for a moment before answering. "You've been overstimulating your mind for years. You need a break. You need boredom. The most important thing right now is that you avoid entering a blue orb at all costs."

Peter nodded. Ever since he came to Tropolis his life has revolved around chasing unnatural pleasures and avoiding the natural pains of life. Luxury had been cruel to him and he realized that his desires, not his hardships had harmed him the most. If he wanted his old self back, if he wanted to enjoy the everyday, normal moments in life, then he would have to sacrifice his supernatural highs. He let out a sigh, "This is going to suck, isn't it." Gregory nodded, "Yes, but it will be worth it."

CHAPTER TEN

A Normal Life

Six months ago Peter was a wretched mess clutching desperately at a broken blue orb. Now he was a changed man. Gregory had given him three gifts to help him on his journey of recovery. A book of maps. A black orb of communication. And a list of people and places that welcomed travellers from all walks of life.

The intricacies of the black orb were far less complex than a blue one and Peter could use it without overstimulating himself. He travelled from place to place meeting new people, learning new skills and doing simple, wholesome work that brought him back into his body. For the first few months, a hopeless energy followed Peter and when he dug a hole or built a fence, he yearned for the satisfaction of slaying an enemy Warlock and wondered if anything in the real world could ever bring him joy again. But in time, the hopelessness dissipated, and he found great enjoyment in these mundane tasks.

The evenings were a challenge. During the day he was surrounded by people and the social bonds kept him in a state of joyful community

But when the sun went down, and he was in his bed alone in the dark, the agony came. The reality of spending seven years trapped inside a blue orb, with no control over himself as he indulged in meaningless pleasures finally dawned on him. And with it came a great pain.

Regret, shame, guilt, disgust, disappointment, sadness and anger visited him one by one and demanded that he looked directly at what he had done and the harm it has caused him. Every lie that he told himself, every wasted moment had to be faced and acknowledged fully. It cut him deep. It made him cry and rage and feel his hurt. The soul feels excruciating pain at even the slightest acts of self harm. And Peter had amassed a lot of debts that needed to be paid.

But he was paying them. Little by little. And it brought him a newfound sense of self respect. Night after night he sat with his pain allowing himself to feel what he needed to feel.

But he knew what he had done. He knew that even if he lived the rest of his life with dignity and honour a single relapse would send him back into the realms of hell.

He felt whole again, but now his constant companion was an intense clarity of just how easy it would be for him to fall from grace.

A Letter from the Author

I am all too familiar with the strange power that blue orb magic can have on one's mind. For anyone who feels stuck in a negative loop with blue orb magic, the following websites will give you the chance to change your environment and gain some perspective on life.

I use workaway, but the other two websites are equally recommended by others.

https://www.workaway.info/

https://www.helpx.net/

https://wwoof.net/